A Gift For:

....

From:

....

Published by Hallmark Gift Books,
a division of Hallmark Cards, Inc.,
Kansas City, MO 64141
Visit us on the Web at Hallmark.com.

Editorial Director: Theresa Trinder
Art Director: Chris Opheim
Designer: Scott Swanson
Production Designer: Dan Horton

ISBN: 978-1-63059-762-7
1KDD1710

Made in China
0618

AN itty bittys® STORYBOOK

THE PRINCESS AND THE PEA

BY JENNIFER FUJITA   ILLUSTRATED BY NICOLA ANDERSON

Most fairytales have a princess or two . . .
it's rare one has none of its own.
But this lovely palace was one of those places
where a queen and a prince lived alone.

One stormy night, they heard a loud knock
and found a lone traveler there.
Her clothes were all ragged, muddy, and torn,
and water dripped down from her hair.

"Hi, I'm a princess," the traveler said,
"and I'm really far from my home.
Could I come in and get out of this rain?
I'm soggy and soaked to the bone."

Once she was dry and warm by the fire,
the new girl turned out to be fun.
They ate castle cakes and played toss-the-crown
'til everyone started to yawn.

Was she really a princess? The queen didn't know.
Could there be some way to test?
She had an idea! "Just give me a sec . . .
then you can go get some rest."

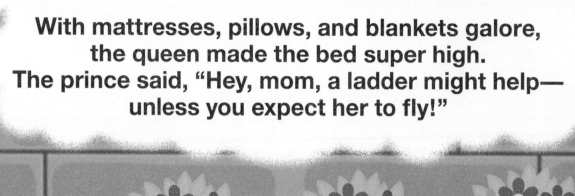

With mattresses, pillows, and blankets galore,
the queen made the bed super high.
The prince said, "Hey, mom, a ladder might help—
unless you expect her to fly!"

The queen said, "I'll put something under the mattress
that only a princess could feel.
If she can't sleep, we'll know soon enough
whether this girl is for real.

How 'bout a melon? Nope, way too big.
An apple? A kiwi? Not quite.
Wait, here's a pea—it's just what we need.
There! Now let's all say good night!"

The very next day, the queen couldn't wait
to see how the traveler had slept.
"Good morning, my dear. How was your night?"
she questioned her overnight guest.

The traveler yawned and rubbed at her eyes.
"Terrible, thanks," the girl said.
"I just couldn't sleep; I tossed and I turned!
It's like there are rocks in that bed!"

"Hooray! So it's true!" the queen and prince cried.
"You're just the princess we need!
If only you'd live here and help rule the land,
we'd make a great kingdom indeed!"

A banquet was held to welcome their guest
and share the incredible news.
"Sure," yawned the princess, "I'm happy to stay . . .
but first, can a girl catch a snooze?"

A princess knows royalty comes from the heart
and not from the crown on her head.
And peas are all right for dinner sometimes . . .
just keep them away from your bed!

If you enjoyed these itty bittys
and the story that they told,
then we would love to hear from you,
our readers young and old!

···

Please send your comments to:
Hallmark Book Feedback
P.O. Box 419034
Mail Drop 100
Kansas City, MO 64141

···

You can also write a review
at Hallmark.com,
or e-mail us at
booknotes@hallmark.com.